Texting with...

Cleopatra

An Ancient Egypt Biography Book for Kids

Written by Bobby Basil

Copyright © 2019 Bobby Basil
All Rights Reserved.

This is a work of creative nonfiction. It is inspired by the life of the subject. It is not an encyclopedic account of events and accomplishments of the subject's life.

No part of this publication may be reproduced or transmitted in any form or by any means except for your own personal use or for a book review, without the written permission from the author.

3 FREE BOOKS!

Go to historytexting.com!

Hi! I'm Alex!

I'm nine, and I don't know what I want to be when I grow up.

There are so many amazing things to do!

My mom helps me text with important people and ask them questions about their lives.

It's fun to ask questions!

Today
my mom and I are
texting with...

Cleopatra!

Cleopatra was a
ruler of Ancient Egypt
that lived from 69 BC until 30 BC.

She was the
last ruler of Egypt before the
Roman Empire.

I can't wait to text her
my questions!

Hi Cleopatra!

Hi Alex!

Thank you for texting with me.

You're welcome.

What do you look like?

I look like this...

Where were you born?

I was born in Alexandria, which was in the Ptolemaic Kingdom.

I've never heard of the Ptolemaic Kingdom before.

It was a kingdom that started from Ancient Greece.

"When I was born, the center of the kingdom was in Egypt."

"Ooh! So you grew up in Ancient Egypt? Did you live with mummies and sleep in tombs and stuff?"

"No, Alex. I think you may have been getting some wrong information. We did have mummies, but our civilization was very advanced."

"So you never slept in a tomb?"

"No."

That's too bad. They're so spooky!

I actually slept in a palace, because I was the Pharoah of Egypt.

Is a Pharoah like a princess?

It's better than a princess. As Pharoah, I was like a queen and ruled over everything. My family was royalty, so I was raised with many opportunities other people did not have.

Like what?

"For one, I had my own tutor as a child who taught me about philosophy. And I got to study at the Library of Alexandria."

"That's almost my name!"

"You're right!"

"I love going to the library. I have my own library card. My mom lets me check out as many books as I can carry. I should call it the Library of Me!"

"This was one of the largest libraries in the world."

- The Library of Alexandria had up to 400,000 scrolls you could read.
- You didn't have books back then?
- Books like the kind you check out from the library weren't invented until 1440. Before then, people had to write everything by hand.
- That must have taken a long time!
- It did. And I got to read all of it!

- I learned at least ten languages. And I was the first of my family to learn Egyptian.
- Why didn't your family learn Egyptian? Didn't they live in Egypt?
- They did not have to learn it because all of the powerful people spoke Greek.
- That's cool you were trying to fit in with the people in your kingdom!
- I wanted to bring many countries together.

- A good way to do that was by learning many languages.

- I want to learn ten languages like you.

- It's very good to know more than just one language. You can use it when you travel or to make a new friend.

- My friend Pete has a friend named Pedro. Pedro speaks Spanish. I wish I spoke Spanish so we could talk at lunch.

- I bet Pedro would love to teach you Spanish, and you could teach him English!

- I like that idea! So when did you become Pharoah?

- When I was only seventeen years old. I had a lot of problems to fix as soon as I became Pharoah. There was a drought in Egypt and many people were hungry.

- What did you do?

- I ordered that my government give hungry people food.

That's a nice thing to do!

There were problems like that all the time when I was Pharoah. But a big problem was my brother wanted to rule Egypt.

Uh oh. Big problem.

It was. My brother and I fought over who would get to rule Egypt.

Who won?

"A famous Roman, Julius Caesar, said we should call a truce and be okay sharing the throne."

"How come that guy got to say what happened?"

"He was trying to take over Egypt and had a large and powerful army. We had to listen to him. As Caesar grew more powerful, he let me rule Egypt on my own."

"Why did he do that?"

"He liked me."

> So did you get to rule Egypt forever?

> No. This was a time in history when the Roman Empire was started. Julius Caesar became the emperor of Rome.

> Is that like a Pharoah?

> Yes. Except the Roman Empire was much larger than Egypt. Caesar was more powerful than anyone else on earth.

> It's good he liked you!

"Yes, except many other people wanted his power, so he died."

"Oh no!"

"Power is a strange thing, Alex. People will do very bad things to get it."

"That reminds me of Lloyd. He ran for class president, but he was mean about it."

"What do you mean?"

"He said the person he was running against, Jill, snored in her sleep. How would he even know that?!"

"He spread a rumor?"

"He did!"

"Did Lloyd win the election?"

"No. I went around the school and had students sign something that said Lloyd was lying, and the teachers kicked him out of the election."

"That's very smart."

"People shouldn't try and become powerful by lying and cheating."

"In my time, people did much worse things than lie and cheat to get the thrown of power."

"That's not nice."

"You're right. After Julius Caesar, more men fought over Egypt. In the end, Octavian the Roman emperor won and made Egypt part of Rome."

- I was the last Pharoah to rule Egypt.
- I don't think I would want to be a Pharoah.
- Why not?
- It sounds like you don't have job security. Anyone could take the job away from you!
- That's true.

"Also, my mom's not a queen, so I don't think I could ever be a Pharoah. But I think I'm going to run for class president next year. I liked talking to people when they signed that sheet for me."

"I think you would be a fantastic president. As long as you are fair and decent to the people you represent, then you will do well."

"Thank you for the advice!"

"You're welcome!"

It was fun talking to
Cleopatra!

I think I want to
learn more about Ancient Egypt
and Ancient Rome now.

There are a lot more people
from then
that I can text
to learn more.

I can't wait to text
the next one!

FUN QUESTIONS FOR YOU FROM...
CLEOPATRA

WRITE YOUR ANSWERS IN THE TEXTING BUBBLES!

Do you like to go to the library?

What languages do you want to learn?

What is a problem in your town that you want to fix?

COMPARE AND CONTRAST WITH...
CLEOPATRA

How are you and Cleopatra the same?

_____

_____

_____

_____

How are you and Cleopatra different?

_____

_____

_____

_____

THINKING ABOUT THE LIFE OF...
CLEOPATRA

How did Cleopatra's life make you feel?

_____

_____

_____

_____

Would you want to live a day in Cleopatra's life? Why or why not?

_____

_____

_____

_____

LEARNING FROM...
CLEOPATRA

What did you find most interesting about Cleopatra's life?

_____

_____

_____

_____

What did Cleopatra teach you?

_____

_____

_____

_____

WHAT FIVE W QUESTIONS WOULD YOU TEXT CLEOPATRA?

1. Who _____ ?

2. What _____ ?

3. When _____ ?

4. Where _____ ?

5. Why _____ ?

meme time with...
CLEOPATRA

DRAW A PICTURE THAT DESCRIBES CLEOPATRA'S LIFE!

"Be it known that we, the greatest, are misthought."

- Cleopatra

PLEASE LEAVE A REVIEW ON AMAZON!

Your review will help other readers discover my books. Thank you!

www.ingramcontent.com/pod-product-compliance
Ingram Content Group UK Ltd.
Pitfield, Milton Keynes, MK11 3LW, UK
UKHW050415240426
12048UKWH00020B/1524

9 781798 987735